It's The Easter Beagle, Charlie Brown

It's The Easter Beagle,

Charlie Brown

Charles M. Schulz

SCHOLASTIC BOOK SERVICES
NEW YORK · TORONTO · LONDON · AUCKLAND · SYDNEY · TOKYO

ISBN: 0-590-04200-9
Copyright © 1976 by United Feature Syndicate, Inc. Produced in association with Lee Mendelson-Bill Melendez TV Production and Charles M. Schulz Creative Associates, Warren Lockhart, President. Based upon the Lee Mendelson-Bill Melendez television production "It's the Easter Beagle, Charlie Brown." (© 1974 United Feature Syndicate, Inc.) All rights reserved under International and Pan-American Copyright Conventions. This edition is published by Scholastic Book Services, a division of Scholastic Magazines, Inc., by arrangement with Random House, Inc.

12 11 10 9 8 7 6   0 1/8

Printed in the U. S. A.   09

We've got another one of those great holidays coming up where boys have the opportunity to give presents to pretty girls. You know, big baskets of candy and eggs and all sorts of things. It's a great time of year for getting.

It's not a time for getting. It's a time for renewal — the start of spring.

You're wrong! It's gift-getting season.

What's the matter with you? All you can think about is gimmee, gimmee, gimmee! Get, get, get!

That's called survival, baby!

I got the eggs, sir, just like you asked.

Great! I'll show you how we color eggs, Marcie. You get the eggs ready, and I'll mix up all the colors. And stop calling me "sir!"

All the eggs are fried, sir.
Now how do we color them?

Argh!

It's almost Easter and I have nothing to wear. Look at these shoes. How can I celebrate Easter properly in these shoes?

Hi! We're on our way to the store. We're getting ready for Easter. You know. We need Easter baskets, eggs, candy—the works. Do you want to join us?

It's a waste of time. The Easter Beagle does all that. On
Easter Sunday the Easter Beagle passes colored eggs to all
the good little kids.

Ooooooh! Linus, you drive me crazy!

The Easter Beagle? Are you
sure, Linus?

Come on, Sally. I thought you wanted to get some
new shoes.

Hi, Chuck! What are you up to? Marcie and I are here to get some eggs to color for Easter.

I told you it's a waste of time to buy and color eggs because the Easter Beagle will do all of that.

Hey, Chuck. What's all this about an Easter Beagle? Has your friend here got all his marbles? He did say "beagle," didn't he?

Well, yes . . .

Come on, Chuck. Let's go in and buy some eggs. Easter Beagle, indeed!

It's Easter and they already have the Christmas decorations up!

Good grief!

I can't believe it!

I told you it's
gift-getting season.

Aren't those shoes a little high for you, Sally?

Maybe. But I like them that way.

Every Easter the Easter Beagle comes dancing along with his basket full of eggs which he hands out to all the good little children.

That sounds faintly familiar. I remember sitting out in a stupid pumpkin patch all night waiting for the Great Pumpkin to come. And he never did. That was the worst night of my life!

This is different. That was Halloween. This is Easter.

Well, I don't know. I really want to believe you because I like you, and I really respect you. But I just don't know.

The Easter Beagle will never let you down.

I know *he* won't. But what about you?

This time, Marcie, *don't fry* the eggs.

I won't, sir.

Hi, Peppermint Patty! Hi, Marcie! Where are you two going in such a hurry?

We keep running out of eggs. I'm trying to show Marcie here how to color eggs for Easter Sunday.

You're making a mistake. All this is a waste of time. The Easter Beagle will take care of it all.

Really?

Sure. On Easter Sunday the Easter Beagle brings eggs to all the little children.

Sir, is he right? Perhaps we don't have to go to all the trouble of making colored eggs if this Easter Beagle is going to do it.

Look, I'm having enough trouble without your crazy stories! Come on, Marcie. Let's go get another dozen eggs.

It's a waste of time....

Now look, kid. These eggs are not to be fried, roasted, toasted, or waffled. These eggs gotta be boiled. You boil them, and I'll show you how to paint them.

Yes, sir. I'll boil them. Then you paint them.

They look done, sir. Do you want to look at them?

Okay, Marcie. Let me look. That's funny. It smells like soup.

MARCIE! YOU'VE MADE
EGG SOUP!!!

ARGH!

Chuck, I don't know what to do. We've ruined three dozen eggs, and we don't have any colored yet. I've run out of money and can't buy any more eggs. How am I gonna teach my friend here about Easter and coloring eggs when I can't get any more eggs to color?

Don't worry a thing about it. The Easter Beagle will come, and you'll see. He'll bring Easter eggs to all the little kids.

Kid, I hope you're right. I don't want my friend here disappointed.

She won't be. On Easter Sunday the Easter Beagle will brighten everyone's day. Everyone will be filled with great warmth and friendship.

You're not coloring Easter eggs, Lucy, are you! You're wasting your time. The Easter Beagle does all that.

Leave me alone. Don't bother me with your stupid ideas. Easter is very simple. You paint the eggs. You hide the eggs. You find the eggs.

And you know who's going to find *these* eggs?...Me! Because I'm the one who's going to hide them!

Well, Marcie. I'm really sorry. Here it is Easter, and we don't have any colored eggs.

I'm the one who's sorry, sir. I guess I'm not much of a cook.

I've seen this happen on holidays before. You look forward to being really happy, and then something happens that spoils it all.

You've done it again, haven't you? I've been waiting here since dawn—waiting for the Easter Beagle. I never learn! Why do I always listen to you? "Trust me," you said. "Trust me! Trust me!" Now I've been burned again!

LOOK! HE'S COMING! HE'S COMING! THE EASTER BEAGLE IS COMING! I TOLD YOU HE'D COME! ! !

Thank you!

Thank you!

Thank you, Easter Beagle! Thank you!

Thank you very, very much!

See! Linus was right! There *is* an Easter Beagle!

Some Easter Beagle!
He gave me my own egg!

What do we do with the Easter eggs now that we have them, sir?

We eat them. We put a little salt on them, and we eat them.

C-R-U-N-C-H!

Tastes terrible, sir.

Still moping? I can't believe it! That was almost ten weeks ago!

I can't help it. I'll never
get over it! NEVER! ! !

Why don't you go
and talk it over or
something?

I guess I will.

All right, Beagle. Come down and we'll have it out!

Come on, Beagle. Put up your dukes!

The Easter Beagle!